First American Edition 2020
Kane Miller, A Division of EDC Publishing

Copyright © 2018 by Makiko Toyofuku
First published in Japan in 2018 by BL Publishing Co., Ltd., Kobe,
under the title *Odoritaino*.
English translation rights arranged with BL Publishing Co., Ltd.
through Japan Foreign-Rights Centre.

Library of Congress Control Number: 2019954834

Manufactured by Regent Publishing Services, Hong Kong, China
Printed August 2020 in Shenzhen, Guangdong, China
2 3 4 5 6 7 8 9 10

ISBN: 978-1-68464-130-7

I Want to Dance

Makiko Toyofuku

Kane Miller
A DIVISION OF EDC PUBLISHING

Near the very edge of the forest, there was a building
filled with beautiful music.

The little rabbit always wondered about it.

Until one night, she peeked inside.

Girls in white leotards and skirts were dancing to music.

They looked so beautiful.

"I want to dance, too," the little rabbit whispered.

She gathered her courage, and knocked on the door.

The dancers were amazed.
"Are you here for class?"
"You want to learn ballet?"

The little rabbit nodded.

"A dancing rabbit?"
"Really?"

So many questions!
Suddenly, the little rabbit wasn't quite so sure.

But the teacher smiled, and made room at the barre.

"Now we begin."

With the music, plié, 1, 2, 3 …

Arabesque, 1, 2, 3 …

The little rabbit loved it.
"I am *dancing*," she thought.

Some things were hard.
Some things the little rabbit couldn't do.
Not yet.

But she was the best at leaps and jumps.
(She was a rabbit, after all.)

1, 2, 3 ...

Grand jeté!

The little rabbit's friends were watching.

They wanted to dance, too.

"You all want to learn ballet?"

The friends were brave. The
teacher invited them inside.

Développé, 1, 2, 3 ...

Pas de bourrée, 1, 2, 3 ...

Grand battement, 1, 2, 3 ...

With the music, 1, 2, 3 ...

But one day, things were different.
They were getting ready for a recital.

"I'm sorry," the teacher said. "It's just for big girls."

The little rabbits were disappointed.
Such fancy things!

Then one of the big girls said, "You should
have your own recital."

What a good idea!
A rabbit recital!

It would be fancy, too!

They needed costumes.

And invitations.

*Please Come!
The night of the full moon.
At the great stump
in the forest.*

And so, on the night of the full moon,
the rabbit recital began.

The big girls heard the music. They peeked.
They had never seen such a stage.

"We want to dance, too."

The little rabbit nodded.

And everyone danced together.